Alex

HENRY

JAMES

PERCY

Based on *The Railway Series* by the Rev. W. Awdry

Photographs by David Mitton and Terry Permane for Britt Allcroft's production of *Thomas the Tank Engine and Friends.*

First American Edition, 1993.
Copyright © by William Heinemann Ltd. 1992. Photographs copyright © by Britt Allcroft (Thomas) Ltd. 1992. All rights reserved under International and Pan-American Copyright Conventions. Published in the United States by Random House, Inc., New York. Originally published in Great Britain by Buzz Books, an imprint of Reed International Books Ltd., London. All publishing rights: William Heinemann Ltd., London. All television and merchandising rights licensed by William Heinemann Ltd. to Britt Allcroft (Thomas) Ltd. exclusively, worldwide.

Library of Congress Cataloging-in-Publication Data
Awdry, W.   Gordon and the famous visitor.—1st American ed.   p.   cm.
"Based on the Railway series by the Rev. W. Awdry"—T.p. verso. SUMMARY: When a famous visitor comes to the station, Gordon becomes jealous and risks his dome to get attention.
ISBN 0–679–84764–2 (trade)   [1. Railroads—Trains—Fiction. 2. Jealousy—Fiction.]
I. Awdry, W.   Railway series. II. Thomas the tank engine and friends.   III. Title.
PZ7.A9613Gm 1993   [E]—dc20   92-45569

Manufactured in the United States of America   10 9 8 7 6 5 4 3 2 1

Random House, Inc.   New York, Toronto, London, Sydney, Auckland

GORDON AND THE FAMOUS VISITOR

Random House

It was an important day in the yard.

Everyone was busy and excited, making notes and taking photographs. A special visitor had arrived and was now the center of attention.

"Who's that?" whispered Thomas to Duck.

"That," said Duck proudly, "is a celebrity."

"A what?" asked Percy.

"A celebrity is a very famous engine," replied Duck. "Driver says we can talk to him soon."

"Oh," said Thomas. "He's probably too famous to even notice us."

Just then Gordon arrived.

"Pah," said Gordon. "Who cares? A lot of fuss about nothing if you ask me." And he steamed away.

Later that night, the engines found that the visitor wasn't conceited at all. He enjoyed talking to the other engines till long after the stars came out.

He left early next morning.

"Good riddance," Gordon grumbled.
"Chattering all night. Who is he anyway?"

"Duck told you," said Thomas. "He's
famous."

"As famous as me?" huffed Gordon. "Nonsense!"

"He's famouser than you," replied Thomas. "He went a hundred miles an hour before you were thought of."

"So he says," snorted Gordon. "But I didn't like his looks. He's got no dome. Never trust domeless engines. They're not respectable. I never boast, but I'd say that a hundred miles an hour would be easy for me."

Duck took some freight cars to Edward's station.

"Hello," called Edward. "That famous engine came through this morning. He whistled to me. Wasn't he kind?"

"He's the finest engine in the world," replied Duck. Then he told Edward what Gordon had said.

"Take no notice," soothed Edward. "He's just jealous. Look! He's coming now."

Gordon's wheels pounded the rails.
"He did it! I'll do it. He did it! I'll do it."
Gordon's train rocketed past and was gone.
"He'll knock himself to bits," chuckled
Duck.

"Steady, Gordon," called his driver. "We aren't running a race!"

"We are then," said Gordon, but he said it to himself. Suddenly Gordon began to feel a little strange. "The top of my boiler seems funny," he thought. "It feels as if something is loose. I'd better go slower."

But it was too late.

On the viaduct, they met the wind. It was a teasing wind that blew suddenly in hard puffs. Gordon thought it wanted to push him off the bridge.

"No, you don't," he said firmly.

But the wind had other ideas. It curled around his boiler, crept under his loose dome, and lifted it off and away into the valley below.

Gordon was most uncomfortable. The cold wind was whistling through the hole where his dome should be, and he felt silly without it.

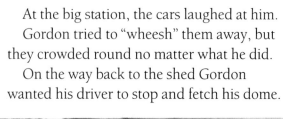

At the big station, the cars laughed at him. Gordon tried to "wheesh" them away, but they crowded round no matter what he did.

On the way back to the shed Gordon wanted his driver to stop and fetch his dome.

"We'll never find it now," said the driver. "You'll have to go to the works for a new one."

Gordon was very cross.
"I hope the shed is empty tonight," he huffed to himself.

But all the engines were there waiting.

"Never trust domeless engines," said a voice from somewhere behind him. "They aren't respectable."

THOMAS

EDWARD

GORDON